T0064682

Casey Calhoun

Casey Calhoun

A Novel

Joseph Sollish

ARCHWAY
PUBLISHING

Archway Publishing books may be ordered through booksellers or by contacting:

Archway Publishing
1663 Liberty Drive
Bloomington, IN 47403
www.archwaypublishing.com
1 (888) 242-5904

ISBN: 978-1-4808-4229-8 (sc)
ISBN: 978-1-4808-4231-1 (hc)
ISBN: 978-1-4808-4230-4 (e)

Library of Congress Control Number: 2017900247

Print information available on the last page.

Archway Publishing rev. date: 01/18/2017

To Claudia, my beloved wife; my three lovely daughters, Erika, Robin, and Bonnie, and their families; my grandsons, Ben, Dan, Michael, and their families; and my great-grandchildren, Freya and Nathaniel. Bless you all!

PROLOGUE

A university can play an important role in many lives, and it can be the very heart of its founders. Although Jason Dermott Phillips University wasn't built until the man whose name it bears had become a paraplegic, it dominates many lives in this story.

Casey Calhoun slept her way to the top of a giant corporation. The many twists and turns of her life, the detours and regrettable mistakes, are the stuff that makes her strong. A long-lost daughter, Clara, given away in infancy to a Swiss family, becomes the object of her motherly love, but meets a surprising and tragic end.

Through it all, her lawyer husband, Paul, stands faithful and supportive of the woman he loves, although some of Casey's misadventures are almost fatal to that love—and him.

This is a family's story. What a family!

CHAPTER 1

I slept my way to the top. From the day I left the family farm in Iowa, I knew that spreading one's knees would work wonders for one's career. I'm Casey Calhoun, president, CEO, and chairperson of the board of directors at Trinitrion Industries Inc.

Sipping Dom Pérignon, I am seated in the company Bentley, being driven from my home in Bel Air to the Bonaventure Hotel. At the wheel is Gregory, my company chauffeur. Seated beside him is Mike Dixon, former FBI, my armed company guard. He is a good lay. So is Gregory. I am an equal opportunity employer.

I hardly notice the buildings we pass—the LA Philharmonic, the Dorothy Chandler Pavilion, city hall, LAPD headquarters. It's all very boring. I am the speaker of the evening at an event sponsored by Trinitrion to raise money for the Cancer Society. My name on the invitation guarantees that companies will buy many tables, each costing thousands of dollars, to further this worthy cause.

When I am finally called to the podium amid a thundering ovation, I deliver my customary address, with a few changes in dates and clichés. The ovation resumes when I finish. As we leave, several strangers come up to me, Mike Dixon on his guard, to offer their congratulations. I couldn't care less.

Arriving home, we pass through the automatic gates, and

2   JOSEPH SOLLISH

Mike does his usual security check of the house as I prepare for bed. He lingers a while but, probably realizing that he won't be invited into my bedroom tonight, goes off to his room next door. I'm very tired and fall asleep rather quickly, instead of enduring my usual restlessness.

———※———

Trinitrion Industries is an international corporation with fifteen subsidiaries around the world. It is a $480 million business, making everything from women's sanitary napkins to army tanks. Its board of directors consists of seven men and two women, and Marianne Childress and me. Marianne has been on the board for ages. A wealthy widow, she spends most of her time on the boards of several companies. She is at Trinitrion so often that she has her own office on the executive floor. Marianne works hard for the generous stipend we pay her, being on more committees than any other member, and chairing the powerful Executive Compensation Committee. She is my only ally.

Executives from other companies make up most of the board. Alan Weisberg, CEO of Simpson Electric, is the most senior—and most vocal—member. He is also my fiercest opponent. Then, among the more prominent members, we also have William O'Toole, a retired naval officer, and Julio Perez, formerly of the Mexican government.

Trinitrion has been criticized for the lack of women on the board and all through the company. The only female senior executive among our subsidiaries is Carla Shelton, who was a vice president at Leukens Steel when we acquired it. I wonder how she made it so high.

The women's issue comes to a head with a lawsuit filed by the teachers union, supported by several militant women's organizations. I steer a motion through the board, despite vigorous opposition, in which Trinitrion agrees to alter the imbalance and get these ladies off our neck.

I immediately seize the opportunity to bring more women into the company. Some of our board members are openly hostile toward the idea—and me. But I am quite successful in attracting capable females for executive positions at Trinitrion headquarters, and I force our subsidiaries to do the same. I put my greatest efforts into placing women into human resources departments, where they can have the strongest influence on hiring practices. They also become my supporters, and I can certainly use a few.

In addition to the women's issue, Wall Street has pilloried Trinitrion for having old fogies on the board, and put the company on the sell list, causing our stock to slump.

The traders are right, of course. Anyone who can read our annual report knows we have several members pushing eighty, a few in their early seventies. After much argument, a resolution is passed: when a member reaches his or her seventy-fifth birthday, he or she will leave the board. Wall Street is pleased to hear this. We're back on their buy list. Trinitrion's stock surges from sixty-five to seventy-three dollars overnight. Executives throughout the company who have stock options make a killing. That includes me.

———————

Marianne Childress takes me aside in the ladies' bathroom.

"Dear," she says, after checking the stalls to be sure we're alone, "I think you should know there's a conspiracy going on."

She has all my attention.

"Yes, dear," she says, "Weisberg, Ashwood, and Perez are working up support to have you removed."

Sure enough, the trio makes such a proposal. Ashwood is the leader. We discuss the motion. I politely ask Ashwood when his birthday is, already knowing he is seventy-eight. I smile.

"Sayonara," I say.

CHAPTER 2

P aul Ellsworth, a senior partner at the law firm of Mittman, Ellsworth, and Fields, is a man I've known for many years. He is also my frequent—and only—partner in bed.

When I find myself pregnant, he has me arrange a tour of our subsidiaries as a reason for being away from Trinitrion headquarters for an extended time. We fly to Switzerland, and that becomes home base while we see Europe. Lots of Europe.

I give birth at Saint Joseph Hospital in Bern, and the infant is immediately put into adoptive care of a Swiss family. I arrange for generous support of the child from a numbered account at a Swiss bank.

———

My campaign to have more women at Trinitrion has been paying off in many ways, chiefly in strengthening my hold on the top job. It has also given me heavy support for measures affecting the subsidiaries. Some very capable women may soon break their own glass ceilings. I don't know how many keep their legs crossed.

———

Walking across the lobby of Agrelli Mills, our subsidiary in

Milan (I'm always on the go), I am accosted by a gray-bearded man wearing a homburg. Mike Dixon is immediately protective.

"*Scusi*, Signora Calhoun," the man says with a slight bow, doffing his hat. He hands me a business card. He is an *avvocato*, a lawyer, from Milan. Valentino Parente.

"Yes?" I ask.

He does the humble act, saying, "Could the signora possibly come to my office? Tomorrow? It is but a small distance from here."

I suggest he tell me what this is all about, right there, if it's not a state secret. He insists that his office would be more suitable. I yield. We will meet at ten in the morning.

Seated behind a beautifully carved mahogany desk in a spacious, well-furnished office, Parente offers coffee, which Mike and I decline. The lawyer opens a thick folder and studies it.

"Signora Calhoun," he asks, "the name Bleckstein, it is known to you?"

"Bleckstein?" I ask. "No, I don't know anyone by that name."

He glances down at the folder. "Gustave Bleckstein? Of Bern, Switzerland?"

Now he has my fullest attention. Bern is one city I'd like to forget.

He closes the folder and folds his hands over it. "Signor Bleckstein would like to know when you will come take your daughter. He lost his wife and cannot take care of the child. He is in ill health."

I see Mike snap to attention at the mention of a daughter, and he stares at me, mouth agape.

"Look, Parente," I say angrily, "you can tell your Mr. Blipstein or Bernstein, whoever he is, to go to hell! I have no daughter, and if this is some kind of scam, I'll get Interpol to take care of him! And you, too!"

I get up and leave, walking so fast Mike has to run to catch up with me. He starts to speak when we are in our car, but I cut him off.

"I don't want to talk about it!" I say. "Forget it!"

CHAPTER 3

Crayton and Associates is an international detective firm that has done some work for me in the past. As soon as I get home from Italy, I call their local office and make an appointment to see John McDermott, one of their top people.

Over coffee in his office, I give John the assignment: find out everything about the Bleckstein child. I know she's the daughter I gave away, but I want to know where she has been, where she is now, everything they can discover. And it's top secret all the way. Mike Dixon is the only person this side of the Atlantic with any knowledge of Clara Bleckstein.

While waiting for the first report from Crayton, I think back to those days with Paul, how loving and caring he was when we toured Italy, France, Germany, and England during my pregnancy, and how he took care of everything in Switzerland when I gave birth. I never knew what arrangements he made on my behalf.

When McDermott calls me, I hurry to his office, where I find his desk covered with documents and photographs. The photos grab my attention. I figure that the girl shown is in her late teens, which John confirms, but what a mess she is! She is round-faced, pudgy, dumpy, and has thick legs—a most unattractive person. I remember what Paul looked like, so she couldn't have inherited it from him. Certainly not from me, either. That good Swiss cooking may have given her that awful shape.

Clara Bleckstein has graduated from a very exclusive school in Lucerne. She is eighteen—was it really that long ago?—and plans to travel to Hollywood to study filmmaking and become a director, the report says. She is due in the United States next month. I certainly don't plan to be her welcoming mother!

———⁓⁓⁓———

Preparations for still another Wall Street presentation occupy all my attention now. In New York, the assembled traders applaud Trinitrion's women's program again when I divulge the statistics on its progress. In addition, the traders give us high marks for changing the old-fogey image of the board. It is a very successful presentation.

During our final banquet in New York, Tom Williams, a young trader sitting next to me, talks about the way some corporations have recently been investing heavily in advertising, which has helped improve their stock positions. He emphasizes "corporate" advertising, not the garden variety of ads promoting merchandise. Trinitrion, Tom says, should seriously think of creating a "corporate image."

I think about it. And I come up with a grand scheme, which I present at our next board meeting. Trinitrion will develop a corporate advertising campaign, but instead of hiring an advertising agency and paying big fat commissions, we will do it all ourselves, with our own in-house agency!

After much discussion, my recommendations are approved, as I expected, especially with the new makeup of the board. My first call is to Martina Custer to have lunch with me at the Four

Seasons. She is a prize-winning copywriter whose career has interested me as an example of women's progress in still another business. She has been a vice president at major agencies, heading up creative departments producing many fine campaigns. And she is thrilled by my offer to be chief of her own agency at Trinitrion.

———✦———

Wasting no time, I clear out an entire floor of our building (we're on all forty-seven floors) and create the space needed for our agency, guided by Martina. She has already done her talent and administrative hiring, so several art directors and producers start filling their places even before the paint dries.

Before long, Martina is ready for the presentation of her first campaign. I have arranged it so I'm her only audience, not wanting a lot of approvals just yet. She has tape mock-ups that tell me she's on the right track.

When Martina presents the campaign idea to the board, it sails through in no time at all. Soon she and a small army of cameramen and producers head out for a tour of every Trinitrion subsidiary (thirty-seven, at last count), to bring back material for the campaign.

As the technical work proceeds, when Martina's group returns, she appears at my office one morning.

"I have a change I'd like to make," she says, "if you agree."

"Which is?" I ask.

"Instead of an announcer-type voice-over," she says, "I think we should have an on-camera spokesman, preferably the president of Trinitrion."

I grin. "You trying to butter me up?"

She seems surprised. "I thought you were just the chairman of the board. I didn't know—"

"That's okay," I say. "I like the idea. Got a script?"

CHAPTER 4

S ignor Valentino Parente, the *avvocato* in Milan, sends me an invoice "for services rendered." I don't know whether to laugh or what. Then, after giving it some thought, I decide to pay the bill, lest he make trouble for me. He could. And would. What's another $800 USD?

By rare coincidence, Martina interviews Clara Bleckstein, who has applied for a job in the production department! Martina doesn't tell me, of course, not having a clue about the girl, but I catch sight of somebody who looks like the photos I've seen (there couldn't be two!) and find it's Clara, for sure.

I must do something for her. I have a conversation with Martina about how we should give novices a chance to get some work experience, "especially women." She says she'll see what she can do, and thinks it's a good idea.

Being a spokesman in a TV commercial isn't as easy as it sounds. I take a long time to get my script memorized (can't stand teleprompters or cue cards) and Martina becomes a little impatient with me. But we get my contribution "in the can," finally, and the rest is up to the sound guys and producers.

Clara gets her chance! Martina is creating six ten-second IDs as part of the corporate campaign and decides to give a few novices a crack at them. She calls Clara. I just happen to pass by our audio room as Clara enters, and I sit next to the sound console while she directs the commercial. I watch through the window.

Clara has learned a lot at the film school, and directs the crew like a pro. She knows all the commands, and barks them as though she's been directing for years.

When I finally hear her shout, "Okay, that's a wrap! Good show, guys!" I leave. I casually inform Martina that I just watched one of her novices direct, and she did a good job.

———————

Our subsidiaries are not happy with the campaign even before they receive their preview reels. Their managements object to being "charged" for corporate advertising that takes money away from their product promotion. This subsidiary allotment is how I plan to pay for the corporate campaign, so I just ignore the griping. Big mistake.

I have underestimated the power of Trinitrion's subsidiaries. They stir up more trouble than I have ever faced. Before long, I find myself in the midst of a pitched battle in the boardroom, defending the corporate campaign. I am attacked for the high costs of production, the salaries and expenses of the in-house agency, the lower-than-estimated amount saved on commissions, *and* the high costs charged to the subsidiaries.

Our Accounting Department does a PowerPoint presentation of balance sheets. Money talks. The board votes. I take the worst beating of my entire career. The corporate campaign is killed. The in-house agency is dissolved. I am censored, by vote, for antagonizing Trinitrion's subsidiaries.

CHAPTER 5

I hole up in my house and remain incommunicado for days, pondering how I went wrong—and feeling sorry for myself. Drinking doesn't help. I'm just as sad drunk as I am sober.

Late one evening, I'm not sure what day it is, I hear the gate buzzer. I stagger out to the intercom and mutter, "Yeah, who the hell is this?"

"Paul," a voice answers, "Paul Ellsworth. Remember me?"

It takes a while for the words to register in my soggy brain. I press the button to open the gates. I hear a car drive in and the gates swinging shut. I go to the door.

When I open it, Paul Ellsworth holds out his arms and gives me a strong hug. I'm not responsive.

"Casey, Casey," he says, holding me tightly. "It's been so long!"

Unsteady on my feet, I lead him into the living room. We sit in the two club chairs near the fireplace. I slump, eyes half-closed.

"Mind if I make myself a drink?" he asks, going to the sidebar. He chuckles. "I won't ask you to join me."

I hear ice cubes falling into a glass, liquor pouring. He returns. Standing in the space between our chairs, he takes a swig of his drink, and then says, "I called your office. They said they haven't seen you for a while, had no idea where you were."

"Just taking a little break," I say, slurring my words. "Fix me a Chivas?"

Paul says, "Sure thing." He goes back to the sidebar. "Johnny Walker okay? You're out of Chivas."

I don't respond, but I hear him make my drink. He brings it to me. I take a swallow. God, am I smashed!

We sit and drink.

"Can you put me up?" Paul asks.

I wave my glass. "Lots of room, lots of room."

"I'll get my bag from the car," he says. He goes off. I hear the front door open. I must have blacked out just then, because that's the last thing I remember.

———

I awaken to the aroma of coffee, the smell of bacon frying. I'm in a nightgown, but I don't recall getting undressed and going to bed. Fuzzy-headed, fighting a hangover, I sit up in bed, trying to get hold of myself.

Paul appears in the doorway, fully dressed, an apron around his waist. "Breakfast? How do you like your eggs? I forget."

I mutter something.

"On the other hand," he says, "one glass of Dr. Ellsworth's world-famous hangover remedy coming up!"

———

Paul helps me straighten up over the next few days. He asks what happened to Lola, the last maid he remembers. There have been several Lolas since he was last here, but I can't recall what happened to the last one.

We're sitting out back, near the pool, basking in the sun, when Paul laughs. "I got the damnedest letter from an Italian lawyer,

actually a bill for services rendered. I don't recall any Italian lawyer being involved with the baby thing, do you?"

The baby thing. His words bring back those last few days in
Switzerland, when Clara was born. I tell him about seeing her,
about her directing the Trinitrion commercial. He's astonished.

"I thought she had become part of a Swiss family," he says.

"That was the deal. Never thought we'd ever hear from her or
about her again."

"Well, she's here, and so far, she hasn't a clue about me, but
who knows what could happen?"

———⁓⟋⟋⟋⟋⟋⟋⟋———

I finally return to Trinitrion. Nobody questions where I have
been all this time. I'm still chairman of the board but no longer
president and CEO. There's no mention of corporate advertising,
either, thank God.

Buried among the mountain of letters stacked on my desk
by Ramona, a new administrative assistant assigned by Human
Resources, I find another invoice from the Italian lawyer,
Valentino Parente. I paid the first one, okay, but now I realize
he's blackmailing me! He could go on bleeding me forever. And
Paul Ellsworth, too. I've got to put a stop to this.

I call John McFadden, at Crayton, the detective agency I've
often employed. I show him Parente's invoice and tell him about
the previous one that I paid. He already knows about the baby,
from the earlier assignment, and agrees that Parente is blackmailing me. He says he'll take care of it, not to worry.

CHAPTER 6

On the front page of *Advertising Age*, a trade paper I started reading when I was involved with Trinitrion's aborted corporate campaign, they have a feature about new campaigns. I can hardly believe my eyes when I see a photo of Clara Bleckstein and read the accompanying article. She is the director of television commercials for Princeton Foods, which, the article states, is certain to win top honors at the next Cleo awards.

She certainly learned fast! The article declares her to be one of the best new directors in the business, and quotes her as saying she would like to direct a feature film in the very near future.

It so happens that I have been approached by Frank Pearson, an independent movie producer, whose films have always been in the running for Oscars. He is looking for backers for a film he wants to make. The wheels start spinning in my mind, making a quick connection between Clara and Pearson.

I talk it over with Paul Ellsworth. He gets a big kick out of it all, that "our" Clara has become such a star. He agrees to handle the legal end of any deal I might make with Pearson.

What I would like to do is tell Pearson I'll put up a big chunk of money for his film, if he has Clara Bleckstein direct it. When I spell this out for Pearson, he immediately accepts the deal, since he is always interested in furthering the careers of new talent.

———⁓᪥⦿ᘐᘖᘗᘐᘖᘗᘐᘖᘗ⦿᪥⁓———

Paul has started a new law firm in partnership with Andrew Carbone, an old Harvard classmate, with offices in one of the twin towers of Century City. It's at Ellsworth & Carbone that Frank Pearson and I put our deal down on paper. Pearson is a boyish guy with sandy hair, a warm smile, and the bluest eyes. I order my bank in Berne to wire Pearson $2,000,000 from my numbered account, which they do the following day. Pearson has said he will get any additional funds needed from other backers. He calls to thank me, saying he will spend the money as though it was his own! I've heard he is adept at bringing in films without astronomical budgets.

Clara is the only hitch. She wants more money than Pearson offers. Our deal is about to go down the drain, when Pearson meets with Clara for the third time and promises to have her direct two more of his future movies. That seals the deal. We're off and running.

When I request a script for the film, Pearson hands me a simple one-page outline! He explains that he prefers his directors and actors to contribute their talent to the fullest, not just execute a rigid, formal script. I guess it's this technique that makes his films so special.

———⁓᪥⦿ᘐᘖᘗᘐᘖᘗ⦿᪥⁓———

The cast and crew leave for Amsterdam, where most of the film will be shot. I intend to follow a few days later, inventing a reason for being away from Trinitrion. But one of my enemies finds out the real reason, and sends the board into a turmoil.

I am told, by a majority resolution, to make a choice: don't go to the filming or resign.

The next day, I board American 136 to Amsterdam.

Good-bye, Trinitrion.

CHAPTER 7

Being a director of a Pearson film has not improved Clara's appearance. She is still pudgy-faced, dumpy, and frumpy, just a little older. But she sure knows how to direct. Despite her looks, she is a commanding presence. I find myself being proud of my daughter!

———

Very little film has been shot, after two days on location in Amsterdam, when an Inspector Mannheim, of Interpol, comes looking for me. I am shocked when he produces a warrant for my arrest as a "material witness" in a homicide. The officer provides no details. I am to be taken to Milan, in manacles, if I show any resistance. Pearson is astonished, as is Clara, who wrings her hands in anxiety.

I call Paul Ellsworth, back in the States, but can only leave a message because of the time difference. I'm already in a prison in Milan when Paul is finally able to reach me. When I tell him what has happened, although I still don't know what this all about, he says he'll get the first flight out, and not to worry.

My Italian jailers treat me courteously, feed me well, and allow me as much privacy as possible, in the circumstances. I try to pry some information from a young guard who has been most attentive to my needs. It's futile, since I know no Italian, and he can barely speak English. All I learn is that it was an *avvocatto,* a lawyer, who was murdered.

Paul arrives, spends some time with me, and then goes off to find out the who, what, when, and where of the case. Hours later, he returns to the jail and tells me the whole story.

The murdered man is our old friend, Valentino Parente. He was found drowned in his bathtub. The Milanese coroner performed an autopsy and declared it a homicide. The police went through Parente's files and found copies of letters to me. Their content led them to believe Parente was blackmailing me, and that I murdered him, or had someone do it for me.

"We can easily prove," Paul says, "that you were nowhere near Milan at the time he was drowned, so that's one charge eliminated." He pauses. "But if they have evidence that you paid an assassin to murder him, they have you as an accessory."

He waits for me to respond, looking around the room the guards have given us. He writes on a pad: "Place may be bugged. Write, don't talk."

What can I write? I ask myself. That I had John McFadden "take care" of Parente? What a mess!

"Have no idea," I scribble on the pad.

He eyes me. "You sure?" he writes.

I nod.

Paul stands. "Well," he says, "see you in court, Hon." He hugs and kisses me, and knocks on the door for the guard to let him out.

Pearson and Clara visit me, both horrified by the turn of events, and promise to keep in touch.

CHAPTER 8

J ail is no place to be, whether it's in Milan or Timbuktu. The guards continue to treat me well, but I'd rather be a million miles from here. They come for me early one morning, to take me to court. I am in manacles, like a common criminal. I am dressed in a baggy orange jumpsuit.

Paul is at a table with two other men, Italians, when I am brought in. The manacles are removed when I sit down next to Paul. My knees are shaking. I had a sleepless night in jail.

After a long delay, the judge, a bearded man in black robes, steps out from behind a black curtain to seat himself on a high platform overlooking the courtroom, as a uniformed man cries out in Italian and everyone rises. When we resume our seats, a man gets up from a table off to one side and reads a document in Italian. A second man, in the corner, translates what was read: the charges against me. "*Cotte d'Assise.*" Murder. After another delay, the judge raps his gavel, says something in Italian, and a man who must be the prosecutor rises to speak. He points at me often.

One of the Italians at our table translates what is said. I'm being described as a brutal murderer with no mercy.

When it's our turn to speak, one of my Italian lawyers addresses the judge. He proclaims my innocence of all charges. His words are translated for Paul and me by another of our lawyers. I'm learning what *giudice* means, also *accusatore* and *colpevole*.

Suddenly, the *giudice* raps his gavel, and the court is adjourned.

Paul spends some time with me in my cell. We ignore the possible bugging and commiserate over my situation. Then he returns to his hotel. That night, I dream that Clara helps break me out of jail.

The trial drags on for three more days. Finally, the *giudice* renders his decision: *Colpevole!* I am guilty! He sets a date for sentencing, three weeks later.

Paul says I could get thirty years in prison, the maximum allowed. He will begin work on an *appello* with his Italian colleagues.

My sentencing is put off while further investigation is conducted.

———

I languish in jail. Late one night, Pietro, the young guard who has been very kind and respectful, enters my cell. I am alarmed, thinking he's come to rape me—I wouldn't mind spreading my legs if that would buy my freedom—but he is on another mission. He has a guard's uniform for me to put on, which I do quickly, and he has me follow him out of the prison, right under the noses of the *carabinieri* guarding outside.

Paul is behind all this, he tells me when he takes charge down the street, having given handsome bribes to Pietro and other guards. I change into a dress in Paul's car, and we drive out of Milan.

With forged passports, we board a plane to London, stay at the International overnight, and leave for LAX in the morning, nonstop.

In my Bel Air bed, Paul and I fall asleep.

CHAPTER 9

B eing an escaped criminal is a terrible condition, expecting to be caught at any moment. Paul and I spend just one night at my house in Bel Air, then pack a small bag for each of us and taxi to LAX so neither of our cars will be tracked to the airport.

Paul books us on a flight to Santiago, Chile, which has no extradition treaty with Italy, using the bogus passports he had bought in Milan. We are Mr. and Mrs. Arnold Waxman, of New Jersey. When we land, I am surprised to see all the snow. It's winter in Chile!

Paul hunts up a Realtor, and we are soon living in a snow-covered furnished cottage in the Providentia community. I am still numb. I don't think I've said more than a dozen words in the past two days.

English is spoken everywhere, and we both know some Spanish, so we have no language problem, once I come out of my coma-like state. Paul is happy to see and hear the old me—he had been worried.

But we are still fugitives, and I keep looking over my shoulder, afraid of being followed. We have not communicated with anyone, lest calls be traced, even though there is no danger of being extradited to Italy. I have no idea about the movie Pearson was producing in Amsterdam.

In a month, we begin to relax and feel free. I apply for a job with Narcopa, a textile company. I'm hired as an administrative assistant in its export division, because I know English. Nothing like starting at the bottom! Paul thinks he will check out the bar requirements and study up on Chilean law, maybe join a firm here.

If I could ski, I'd have more fun, I suppose. Everybody skis. This is snow country, and it's winter here, I keep reminding myself. We still haven't bought a car, for fear of having to sign anything, even our aliases. But finally, we take a chance and apply for driver's licenses, and take another plunge—buying a Toyota Camry for me and a big Buick for Paul.

When I take the license test, they find I need glasses! It's the least of my worries. Lately, I can be sitting absolutely still when I suddenly feel a jolt of heat to the point of breaking into a sweat, and then it's gone. Comes and goes. I stop having my period. Of course, I know what's happening; I just don't want to think my time has come. Menopause! God, I thought Casey Calhoun could be Casey Calhoun forever. Now I'm somebody else that I hardly recognize.

CHAPTER **10**

Life as a different me is painful. I'm jittery, on edge, and given to sudden spells of sadness and tears, on an emotional loop-the-loop. Paul sees what's happening, and is nicer than ever. I think a change of scenery might help, and ask if we can move elsewhere. He says we have to be careful not to go where an extradition treaty with Italy is in effect.

"They're still looking for us, you can be sure," he warns. "You ready to take the risk? Go to jail?"

I shudder. How I wish it could all be over, and my life could be my own again! My old life, actually. But I know that's gone forever.

Frank Pearson, wreathed in a parka, appears at our house! I am flabbergasted. How in the world has he found us? He stamps the snow off his boots, and catches me looking to see if anyone's behind him.

I welcome him in, and he gives me one of his boyish grins. "Looking for Clara? She's at the hotel." He pulls his phone out of a pocket. "I'll let her know; she'll be here in a flash."

Paul is away somewhere. I know he'll be as delighted as I am, but I'm suddenly worried again: if Frank Pearson can find us, how far behind can the cops be?

Pearson sits with me before the flaming fireplace, drinking cocoa with marshmallows. I have a cabernet. He tells me how the film production went in Amsterdam, that they have plenty of footage but still have major scenes to film.

"Clara," he says, "is great. She is one of the best directors I've ever worked with." He adds, "Everybody loves her."

"But how did you find us?" I want to know. "We covered our tracks so well a pack of bloodhounds couldn't pick up the scent!"

"It wasn't easy, not by a long shot," he declares. "I knew you'd look for a country that wouldn't extradite you to Italy, and after a lot of misses, and I mean a lot, we finally hit the old bull's-eye! More good luck than anything."

But if he could do it, so could Interpol, I remind myself once more. Suddenly I'm chilled, though sitting close to the burning logs.

A car pulls into the driveway. I tense for a moment, but Pearson goes to a window and exclaims, "And here she is!"

Clara is wearing a thick, furry coat that makes her look even more stumpy. She gives me a hug, and I feel her still holding me tightly when I'm ready to let go.

"I thought we'd never find you," she says, shedding her coat. "Frank is some bounty hunter!" She kisses him lightly on the lips. *Well, well*, I think, *what have we here?*

We huddle around the fireplace. Pearson puts another log on the fire, sending sparks shooting up the chimney. It's snowing again, I can see in the window—big flakes piling up on the sill. I wonder if Paul is driving in all this. I hate driving in a snowstorm, not seeing where I'm going. How I long to be basking in the sun beside the pool in Bel Air, sipping iced tea!

The evening wears on; still no Paul. "Oh, look what time it is!

I had no idea!" I say, getting to my feet. I'm testing, to see if my guests will indicate where they will spend the night.

Clara goes to the window. "Really coming down," she murmurs. Frank stands beside her, an arm around her waist.

I think I know what they would like to hear. "I can put you up. Not good driving in a snowstorm. It usually gets worse during the night."

Frank turns. "Just show the way," he says. He yawns. "Tired. Been a long day."

I lead them down the hallway. No doubt now that they will sleep together; there's just one guest room. I flick on the light, and check the bathroom for towels.

"Sleep tight," I say. Clara gives me a hug. I return to the living room to wait for Paul.

CHAPTER 11

Clara and Frank Pearson announce they are getting married. I am delighted, and so is Paul. Such an old-fashioned idea these days! Pearson was married once, I know from the fan magazines, to a famous actress, but they divorced after a year or so. Clara looks so happy. I think she is a late bloomer, actually pretty, losing weight along with much of her dumpiness. Never thought I'd see that!

They've taken a house a short distance from ours. We spend a lot of time together, the four of us. Right now, I'm helping Clara plan her wedding. She wants a big one, in a church, with a reception—all the bells and whistles. I'm surprised.

We find a great gown for her, one that makes her an appealing bride. She keeps surprising me with everything she does. I'm so proud. I think I've become a real mother, finally!

Frank Pearson doesn't show up at Santo Domingo church. The priest waits, and the guests in the pews get restless. Paul stands outside on the church steps, in the freezing cold, looking for the groom. Pearson had told Paul, his best man, to go on ahead; he has something to do, but will be at Santo Domingo's with time to spare.

Paul checks with the police, finds there have been no auto accidents in the last few hours. I lead Clara to a small room at the rear of the church. She sits, eyes downcast, hands folded in her lap, a pretty bride in a lovely wedding gown. She cries softly. We sit for another hour. When we walk down the aisle to leave, Santo Domingo is dark and empty.

Paul drives us to our house. We pass Clara's on the way, and it is dark. I help her out of her wedding gown, and prepare her for bed.

"Can I sleep with you?" she asks plaintively. Only the word *Mom* is missing. But that's what it sounds like to me. I hug her and help her into my bed. I pull the blankets up, and tuck her in snugly. I don't remember ever being sung to sleep, but I know that's what moms are supposed to do for their children. Somehow, I have a lullaby in my head, and I sing it to Clara.

Rock-a-bye, baby
In the treetop.
When the wind blows,
The cradle will rock.
When the bough breaks,
The cradle will fall,
And down will come baby,
Cradle and all.

I kiss her on the forehead, click off the light, and tiptoe out.

Paul and I talk about Frank Pearson. Why would a man with his reputation as an unselfish, caring individual, who produces such meaningful films, do such a rotten thing? There has to be some reason. Paul is determined to find it.

CHAPTER 12

Spring arrives in Santiago with the budding of bare, winter-weary trees, while there are still traces of snow on rooftops and roadsides. The peaks of the Andes are white. Clara lives with us now. She has come alive again and talks about going back to Hollywood and resurrecting her career.

I tell her I can't go with her, afraid of being caught by Interpol and taken back to jail in Italy. She appreciates my dilemma, but wants me with her. Paul, ever the entrepreneur, says, "Why not try setting up a film company of your own right here?"

At least, his suggestion gives Clara something to think about. Soon she is on the phone with people back in Hollywood, and a producer, Sam Brockett, flies to Chile to meet with her. They decide to acquire some promising properties, find backers, assemble a crew, and make movies! No unions to worry about and run up costs. Great locations to shoot in. And they don't know it yet, but they have built-in backers: Paul and me!

I receive a letter (addressed to Mrs. Arnold Waxman) on Valentino Parente's stationery! Just the sight of the lawyer's name scares the hell out of me. My hands are trembling as I read the letter.

> My dear Mrs. Calhoun,
>
> Kindly immediately wire $50,000 USD to Account E439876 at Schweizer Bank, Berne, Switzerland, or Interpol will be given your present location and alias.
>
> Sincerely,
> (signed) Valentino Parente

My shakes are still rattling my body when Paul returns from his office. I didn't call him. It's not something to be discussed on the phone.

One look at me, and he knows something terrible has happened. He reads the letter, rereads it, examines the paper, and studies the letterhead.

"Christ!" he exclaims. "Blackmailed by a dead man! What the hell!"

I calm down. We have drinks, sit and think.

"If we pay up," Paul says, "it'll be only a down payment, for sure. If we call his bluff—" He shakes his head. "He knows too much. It's no bluff."

"Then it's time to move on," I state firmly, no longer as frightened as I was just a few minutes ago.

Paul nods. "But let's not jump too fast."

"He says 'immediately,'" I quote from the letter.

We sit for a while longer, and then wordlessly go to our room. Neither of us has a good night's sleep.

CHAPTER 13

Without a word to Paul, I take a chance and call Crayton, the detective agency I've used many times in the old days, and speak with John McFadden. He was very much involved with us in the baby situation in Berne, and later with Parente.

I update him on everything, trusting him because he also could be in trouble with Interpol if they caught me. I tell him about the letter supposedly from the dead lawyer.

"Pure and simple blackmail, of course," McFadden says. "It has to be someone who worked with Parente, or somehow could get at his stationery, his files."

"So will you look into it?" I ask. "Same fee?"

"This one's on the house," he laughs. "I hate blackmailers."

I thank him and end the call. I hope I haven't put us in danger, but we can't let it slide. I don't want to be paying whoever it is for the rest of my life.

Paul isn't too happy when I tell him about my call to McFadden, but finally agrees we have to get to the bottom of this newest mess.

Clara is well into establishing her film production company with Sam Brockett. She has given it a name that has a familiar, but sad, ring to it: Domingo Films. I guess that means she's no longer mourning her "late" husband!

McFadden calls. "Got a name for you," he says. "Jaime Aguilara. Mean anything?"

I say it doesn't. "Who is he?"

"He has, or had, an office on the same floor with Parente. After Parente went bye-bye, Interpol got a little careless, I suppose, and somebody broke into Parente's office. But as far as they could see, nothing was taken." McFadden pauses. "Who knew how many letterheads the guy had? That's what Aguilar made off with."

"And he forged Parente's signature?"

McFadden laughs. "Doesn't matter. Who's checking?"

I wait a while before saying, "Can you take care of Aguilara, then?"

"Consider it done," he replies. "You owe me a beer."

———

News about Domingo Films is reported in various trade papers—*Variety*, *Billboard*, *Hollywood Reporter*. Clara receives calls from talent agencies, lots of scripts, and notices about productions going on. But one letter is from Gustave Bleckstein, her Swiss "father."

She shows it to me. Together, we manage to decipher the scrawled handwriting, the weird English. Bleckstein is asking for some money. He's old and could use her help.

"What should I do?" she asks.

"Send the guy a few bucks," I reply. "After all, he did bring you up."

"American dollars? Should I just mail him cash?"

"Sure," I say, "our money is good everywhere."

I wonder how much Clara remembers of those years, and if

she has ever connected the dots as far as I was involved. I wonder why she hasn't made any effort, as far as I know, to find her real mother, as so many children do when they grow up. But sometimes, when she clings to me, I have a deep-down feeling she knows I'm her mother. Just a feeling.

Clara sends him ten ten-dollar bills. She never hears from Gustave Bleckstein again.

———〜〜〜⚬⚬⚬〜〜〜———

I get another letter from Italy. It's a duplicate of the blackmail one McDermott said Jaime Aguilara sent, except for the date, a month later than the first.

McDermott is puzzled when I call to tell him. "Jeez," he says, "the bastard must have set up some kind of automatic mailing. He sure as hell didn't send this from where he is, believe me."

"Or he's not our guy," I state.

John thinks a bit. "I'll get back to you, Casey."

We end the call. *Christ*, I tell myself, *we can't go around knocking off every Italian who has a fountain pen!*

CHAPTER 14

A ndres Fouillard is tall and lean, with a rich black moustache and a military bearing. He stands at my door, opening a leather wallet to present his credentials. He is an inspector from Interpol. Latin American Division.

I am stunned as if I had been struck by lightning. He sees I am about to collapse and reaches out his arms to steady me.

"May I please come in, Madame Calhoun?" he asks.

Speechless, I step aside to allow him to enter, and then show him into the living room. I've regained my composure and wave him to be seated on the sofa.

"Would you like something to drink?" I ask, my voice strained. I'm alone in the house. It's five in the afternoon, and Paul has phoned that he will be late.

"A glass of water would be fine, if you please," he replies. "Lovely room," he adds, glancing about.

I pour ice water from a pitcher on the sidebar and bring him a glass. He thanks me, takes a swallow, and waits for me to provide a coaster before placing his glass on the end table. I sit on a club chair facing him across a long marble-top table.

"Madame Calhoun," he begins, as I find myself leaning toward him in anticipation, "I would have come sooner, but there was considerable, how shall I say, difficulty in locating you." He smiles. "Your cover has been splendid."

For Christ's sake, I think, *get to the point; clap me in irons and haul me away already.*

"However," he continues, "you have no need to conceal yourself any longer, Monsieur Calhoun either, since we have in custody the individual who committed the crime of which you were accused. The case has been closed. And we beg your pardon for our grievous error."

I can't believe my ears! My first impulse is to throw my arms across the table to embrace him, but I quickly realize he may be talking about John McFadden. Oh, God, no!

"Can you tell me who he is?" I ask, almost shaking again.

"Sorry, Madame Calhoun," he replies, "all I may say at this time is that he is an Italian. And a career criminal."

He stands up, smiling. "And now I must leave. So, adieu, Madame Calhoun, and please give my regards to your husband."

Only his staunch military bearing prevents me from throwing my arms around him. I show him out, feeling foolish as I say, "Au revoir," and watch him drive away.

No one in the world is as happy as I am at this moment. I rush to my phone and call Paul, but I reach only his voice mail. I don't leave a message. I can hardly wait for him to come home. Free! Free at last! I laugh almost hysterically at having thought of Martin Luther King's words.

———

Mr. and Mrs. Arnold Waxman have no reason to exist any longer, and we laugh as we rip up the bogus passports. Paul and I pay our bills, practically give our cars back to the dealers, pack our bags, and prepare to return to Bel Air. Clara is overwhelmed with joy at our freedom, but is teary-eyed when we hug and say good-bye at the airport. I exact a promise that she will come to see us soon.

CHAPTER 15

A year has passed since the whole nightmare of being fugitives ended, and we have settled into the Bel Air house again. Clara has come and gone, twice, looking fine, her company producing several films. I'm trying to persuade her to move back to Hollywood, but she likes being in Chile. She speaks Spanish like a native.

I'm curious about Trinitrion, or maybe it's just because I am bored doing nothing but lounging around the pool, going to theater matinees, visiting the contemporary art museums that seem to be springing up all over Los Angeles. I call Marianne Childress, my old ally on the board. I am told she is at Ocean Gardens Assisted Living, in Santa Monica. I am saddened, but she was already quite old when I worked with her. It's a wonder she is even still living; she must be close to ninety.

But I don't care to see her, now that I know where she is. Just for the hell of it, I ask for Mike Dixon, my ex-FBI personal guard, and I am told that he is at Protective Security, in Pasadena. I Google the company, discover that it has several offices around the country, 130 employees, and Dixon owns it! Good for him!

I'm thinking I could call and see what has happened to Gregory, my company chauffeur, but I don't want to hear that he owns a fleet of Bentleys-for-hire, or something like that, so I cross him off my mental list.

Checking into what's happening with old Trinitrion colleagues doesn't relieve my boredom much, and I call Paul, to see if he's free for lunch. He is senior partner at a new law firm (it must be his third or fourth), Ellsworth, Rubin & Mitchell, in downtown LA.

He's in court all day, I'm told. I go sit at my pool. God, am I bored!

———✦———

Carolyn March calls. The ringing wakes me up from my morning snooze at the pool. When she first mentions her name, I can't place her, but as she talks, I remember. She is the vice president Trinitrion acquired with the purchase of Lexington Steel, becoming the only female executive in the whole corporation, besides myself. We talk old times stuff, although I don't remember our being friends in any way. She invites me to have lunch, and I jump at the opportunity.

We meet at Spago, in Beverly Hills. She has a "regular" table in the open area, I learn, when I tell the girl at the desk that I'm meeting Carolyn March. I'm already seated there when she arrives. She is a good-looking, "mature" woman, blonde, superbly dressed.

Over martinis, I learn that she is on Trinitrion's board, and chairs the salary committee. Wolfgang Puck stops by, addresses her by her first name, and then says, "I remember you!" when Carolyn introduces me. "You the one what got canned, no? Am I right?"

I give him a sickly smile, and he goes off to greet other guests. Carolyn laughs. "What a way to be remembered," she remarks.

We chat about fashion, designers, where I've been, and what's new, and while we dig into our entrees, she asks, "How about coming back to Trinitrion?"

I snort. "As if they'd have me!"

"No," she says. "Seriously, would you?

I shrug. "Okay, I'll give it a whirl."

"Let me work on it and get back to you," she replies, and that ends that discussion.

CHAPTER 16

At Trinitrion, I am asked to wait in the lobby for someone to fetch me, when I tell the guard at the counter I am here to see Ms. March. I grab a *Time* magazine and read it until a young man in a blue suit approaches and asks me to follow him.

The well-groomed young man turns out to be Carolyn's administrative assistant, and he leads me into a room that I expect to be her office. Instead, it's a boardroom, and Carolyn is standing at the head of a long table, where several people are seated. *She is the chairman of the board!*

She greets me with a big smile and introduces me. "Ladies and gentlemen, please welcome Casey Calhoun, at one time chairman of this board." She shows me to a chair at the table and resumes her place at its head.

I am dumbfounded. I sit, trying to collect myself, and finally glance about the table. Not one face do I recognize, and they all seem to be looking at me with curiosity, as if I'm a freak of some kind. Two are African American women; that's new for Trinitrion!

Carolyn calls the meeting to order. Several measures are put to a vote, including one that decides whether "Casey Calhoun shall be a member of Trinitrion's board." I refrain from voting on anything just yet, but the resolution about me passes, with a little applause.

When Carolyn adjourns the meeting, four or five members, men and women, shake my hand, introduce themselves, and welcome me back. Carolyn shows me into her office, passing her assistant's cubicle. His desk nameplate reads: R. Williamson. He nods as we go by.

Chivas Regal, right?" Carolyn asks, poised at the sidebar. I say "Yep," and she pours us drinks. She hands me a current Annual Report to take home, and she talks about the quirks and personalities of some members. When I comment favorably on the presence of African Americans, she says, "Yes, we've moved into the twenty-first century, finally."

When I get home, I'm exhausted, not used to meeting so many people at one time, and listening to so many things I don't understand. I lounge at the pool. It's still summer, so the sun warms me, but then, it's mostly "summer" in Bel Air.

I try Paul; he's still in court. I never seem to get him at the office. I have brought out to the pool a pile of old Trinitrion Annual Reports, to see the yearly changes in management and corporate income. Trinitrion has grown considerably, almost doubled its income, added ten new subsidiaries—become an absolute behemoth, since my days. Could it be the largest corporation in America? In the world?

I wonder if I should go back. I slept my way to the top the first time; this seems too easy. I laugh to myself. *Who would want me to spread my legs for him now? Can't use sex to get what I want anymore, old hag that I am.*

Suddenly I'm feeling sorry for myself. Ridiculous! Here I am, living in a $4 million Bel Air home with a man who adores me, with I don't know how many millions in my numbered Swiss bank account, and on the board of one of the world's largest corporations, yet feeling sorry for myself? *Get with it, gal!*

When Paul comes home, I'm about to prepare dinner. It's my chef's night off. (Yes, we have a real chef, Francois, who can make the most fantastic meals. I hardly cook anymore.) Paul opens a small black box. It's a diamond ring, ten carats at least.

"Will you marry me?" he asks.

All "sorry" vanishes. "Oh, Paul," I say, slipping the ring on my finger, "I thought you'd never ask." I throw my arms around him, and we kiss deeply.

We've been together so long, even have a child, that we decide to just take a holiday and fly to Reno to be married. Now I indeed have everything.

CHAPTER 17

Being on the board of Trinitrion gives me plenty to do, as I volunteer to work on several committees. I particularly like the one concerned with executive compensation. It wields great power, and power is what I like having. I aim to chair that committee before long.

But it won't be easy. My competition is very strong, mainly an older man (well within the age boundaries), Jeff Baldwin, CEO of Maxwell Publishing. It will take time, but I can wait.

Paul and I agree to tell Clara that we are her parents, now that we are in fact Mr. and Mrs. Paul Ellsworth. We should have anticipated her reaction. After all, we've been lying to her all these years. But we are astounded by the force of her reaction.

"You abandoned me!" she shouts, her face red with anger. "You sold me to Gustave Bleckstein! Now you dare claim me as your daughter?"

I don't know what to say. She's right, of course, but doesn't our confession set it straight?

Clara storms out of our house, after her final words. "I don't want to see either of you ever again!"

—⁓⸜∘⸎⊙⸎⸓⊙⸎∘⸝⁓—

The closest we come to Clara is to read news of films she has directed. She has become one of Hollywood's top directors, with two Oscars to prove it.

Her rancor against us is obviously still boiling when she gets married, and our only notice is in the newspapers. That hurts me deeply. In spite of Paul's objection, I send her a silver candelabra wedding present. She sends it back.

But I don't let go. She means much more to me than Paul thought, so he is taken by my attitude and wants to help. He warns me to be careful not to be hurt still more.

I write a note to Clara, inviting them to cocktails and dinner with a few friends at my home. Chef Francois will serve his specialty, *beouf bourgignon*. Surprise! Ben Lintermann, her husband, calls to accept.

Lou and Marcey Hillsworth, Raymond and Meg Goodman, and Perry and Anne Levy are milling about the living room, sipping their cocktails, commenting on our Rothko and Helen Frankenthaler on the walls, when Clara and Ben arrive.

Clara is pregnant, probably in her fifth month! I recover from my surprise and make the introductions all around. Everyone is solicitous of Clara. My latest maid, Erma, carries around a tray of *hors d' oeuvres*. Chef Francois, wearing his tall white hat, summons us to the dining room, where a centerpiece of pink lilies graces the table. The wine flows, the talk is involving, the *boeuf bourgignon* an absolute triumph. Coffee and *crème brulee* end the dinner. Clara has been warm toward me and Paul all evening. I hope it lasts beyond tonight.

I test the waters by calling Clara to have lunch with me. After several attempts, we finally connect and have lunch at Captain Hook's, near Paramount, where she has been viewing a rough-cut with studio executives. All my transgressions seem to have been forgotten or forgiven, and we have a pleasant hamburger lunch. I caution her, in a motherly way, to lay off the fried onions, and she smiles.

———∿∿✦⊙❧✦∿∿———

Ben Lintermann calls me when Clara is rushed to Cedars-Sinai, and I am with her hours later when the infant, swathed in a blanket, is placed in her arms. Clara smiles wearily at me as she holds her tiny son.

Paul and I are invited to Carla's home in the Hollywood Hills for the baby boy's *bris*, his circumcision, which must be done on his eighth day. Carla presents us to the *mohel* who performs the ritual as the baby's grandparents, and Grandpa Paul is enlisted to help. It seems a bit barbaric to me, but it's a happy occasion for the house full of guests, who enjoy wine and *hors d' oeuvres*. The event is most meaningful to me because Clara has called us the child's grandparents. *We are family.*

CHAPTER 18

Now the business world no longer dominates my life. I find myself spending far more time with little Aaron than with giant Trinitrion. Carolyn March calls this to my attention impatiently.

"I went to a lot of trouble," she reminds me, "to bring you back. So what will it be?"

I apologize for neglecting my work, and promise to mend my ways, which means attending meetings of the board, and working on the Remuneration Committee. But I would rather be running around Saks and Neiman Marcus looking for cute baby clothes than sitting on my ass in a meeting.

Ultimately, the doting grandma act costs me my job. "Sorry," Carolyn says, "I can't let this continue. You're fired."

That's how my career at Trinitrion ends. Again.

Clara has put her directing career on hold. Taking care of little Aaron is her full-time job. I spend much of my time with them, and baby-sit when Clara has to go out. I love pushing Aaron around in his carriage. People stop me to peek in at him. I'm so proud.

—⁓⦿⦾⦿⦾⁓—

I get a call from a Lawrence Metcalf, who says he knows me from Trinitrion, but I can't place the name. He has a proposition he'd like to discuss. He won't give me any details over the phone, so out of curiosity, if nothing else, I agree to take a lunch with him.

We meet at Morton's. I don't remember him at all. He's tall and bald, and talks in a loud voice as if he's hard-of-hearing.

Why he called me, I'm not sure, because his proposition is risky as hell, and illegal. Maybe I have a reputation for shady dealing that I don't know about!

It involves redirecting certain imported merchandise by altering the destination on bills of lading as the goods enter the United States, then collecting and selling them on the black market at a 100 percent profit. What he needs from me is financial backing to pay off the many import-export officials he must bribe. The split would be 60/40, in my favor. "It could mean millions," he says.

Do I want to get involved in a crooked scheme? I could use the money, I know, since my income is zero, and the balance in my Swiss account is dwindling. I've taken a bad hit in the market, too. We are thinking of getting a second mortgage on the Bel Air house.

I tell him I'll get back to him. I want to talk with Paul.

—⁓⦿⦾⦿⦾⁓—

"Are you out of your fucking mind?" Paul yells when I tell him about Metcalf's deal. "You could get twenty years!"

I back off, feeling pretty stupid, being yelled at like this by my husband. I guess it's the lawyer in him that makes him react so strongly.

"Okay, okay," I say sheepishly. "I just asked. No need to take my head off."

But the lure of 100 percent profit and the 60/40 split is too strong. I talk with Metcalf again, this time at a Denny's in Hollywood. I'm in.

———

Our first go takes place the following month. Everything works the way Metcalf described, not a single hitch. It takes another month for the goods (I'm never told just what they are) to be sold off. Metcalf hands over a suitcase containing $45,000 in cash! I hide it while I figure out what to do with the money.

The next time we do the deal, I am told the shipment is high-end fabrics worth hundreds of thousands. The goods are sidetracked as before, collected, and then sold off.

When Metcalf drives me to a house in Santa Monica where we're to make the split, we are met by three men in blue suits, pointing pistols at us.

"FBI! Put your hands up!" one shouts.

Shaking, I raise my hands. Metcalf moves over beside the agents.

"Okay, fellas," he says, "let's wrap it up."

An agent pulls my hands down behind my back and claps handcuffs on my wrists. Metcalf gives me a half smile as I am hustled out to a waiting SUV and driven away.

CHAPTER 19

This is not the first time that Paul has visited me in jail, but it's the first time he is so furious with me.

I sit on the bed, my head in my hands, eyes down. I can't face him.

"What the hell!" he shouts. "I told you to stay out of this, and do you listen? Do you realize what you walked into? A sting! An FBI sting operating under this Metcalf guy, Special Agent Metcalf!"

I have nothing to say.

"Twenty years, Casey," Paul says, no longer shouting. "You could be in prison for twenty years. Has that sunk into your feeble brain?"

I finally look up. "I'm sorry, Paul," I croak. "I … I don't know what I can say." I sway back and forth, back and forth. "Stupid, stupid, stupid."

Paul sits down on the bed beside me and swings an arm around my shoulders. I bury my face into his chest and cry.

———

At my arraignment, I plead "not guilty," and I'm returned to my cell, pending a bail hearing the following day. Paul posts bail of $50,000 and surrenders my passport, and the judge sets trial for two months from now.

Clara has not been in the court, but she hurries to my house when Paul phones her that I'm out on bail. She is doleful but tries to cheer me up by talking about her child.

"You should see how Aaron has grown!" she exclaims.

"How is he?" I ask.

"Oh, fine, fine," she says. "He's actually starting to crawl!"

I'm thinking he'll be going to college by the time I get out of prison. Nice, having a jailbird for a grandma.

————⟊⟊◦◦⟋◦◦⟊◦◦⟋◦◦⟊⟊————

Paul discusses the case with his law firm partners and tells me, "We think we'll plead entrapment, that you were set up to take the fall by the FBI. That's not allowed, illegal."

"You think it will work?" I ask, hopeful.

"It's up to the jury," he answers. "Anyway, there isn't another defense we can use."

We're sitting at our pool in Bel Air, relaxing with glasses of iced tea. It's hard to imagine that one of us could be going to prison. I start thinking about the fake passports we used to escape to Chile. I can't remember the name. Arnold? Maxwell? Something like that. What if I used that passport to escape jail again? I could be on a plane and gone before anyone knew!

Looking over at Paul, who has fallen asleep in his chaise, I sigh, knowing what he would say. Wow, he'd lose the bail he put up, $50,000! And he'd tell me I'm insane. Insanity! Wouldn't insanity be a good thing to plead instead of entrapment?

Paul stirs, awakens. He looks over at me. I don't dare even to broach the subject.

CHAPTER 20

L ooking over the jury that finally has been selected, after three
days of questioning and accepting and rejecting, I try to find
a friendly face. Who knows what they'll decide when the time
comes? Our jury-selecting specialist thinks he does. I can only
pray he's right.

The prosecutor, a young assistant district attorney, character-
izes me as a "greedy, avaricious person who lives in a mansion in
Bel Air and commits crimes to support her lavish lifestyle."

When it's our turn to make an opening statement, Paul char-
acterizes me as an innocent, naïve woman who has been entrapped
by ambitious FBI agents.

The trial lasts five weeks, including two adjournments for the
judge to handle some other legal matters, and another to replace
a juror who has a heart attack. Six FBI agents are called to give
testimony against me, including the one who set me up, Metcalf,
the bastard. The prosecutor also questions workers who verify bills
of lading at various ports.

We have no witnesses of our own to call, but Paul re-calls
Metcalf and questions him endlessly about the sting, and why he
chose me for the unwitting victim. He puts me on the stand with
similar questions. I'm scared stiff. When Paul is satisfied that he

has proven I was the innocent sufferer of a vile entrapment, he ends his presentation of the defense.

I hardly hear the closing statements. When the judge turns the case over to the jury, Paul almost has to carry me to the car, I am so limp with anxiety.

It takes the jury just under two hours to reach a decision. When it is read by the foreman, I pass out, and drop to the floor like a stone.

"Not guilty!"

I don't remember going home. I don't remember undressing. I don't remember going to bed.

I sleep for the next eighteen hours.

CHAPTER 21

Clara shares her son with me unselfishly, driving to Bel Air almost every day, with Aaron strapped securely in the baby seat. We sit out at the pool, basking in the sun, while Aaron naps in the portable cradle. When he wakens and cries, Clara gives him his bottle, or picks him up to sit on her lap so I can fuss over him. I think he likes me. He smiles a lot.

Clara had boasted some time ago, before the trial, that Aaron was starting to crawl. But one day, we are keeping close eyes on him as he crawls about on the lawn surrounding the pool, when he suddenly struggles to stand up and takes a few tottering steps!

We both rush to catch him as he falls, Carla hugging him and saying, "Oh, what a big boy you are, Aaron! Mama's boy is walking!"

Before long, he is scampering—well, tottering fast—around the lawn, with his mother and me watching him closely. I'm afraid he'll go for a swim!

The Lintermanns have dinner with us at least three times a week, and they often drop Aaron off at our house in the evening when they have tickets for a play or a concert. Ben is difficult to get to know. He has little to say; an introvert, he borders on being just plain dull. He is a vice president at California Bank, so maybe that explains it. Paul tries to draw him out, with little success. But Clara is very much in love with her husband, and he adores her, so that's all that matters. Everybody can't be blabbermouths like Paul and me.

I'm visiting them in their house high up in the Hollywood Hills one afternoon. I don't do this very often, because the roads up to the house are so winding and steep. Aaron is napping. We're having tea with tiny wafers Clara has baked.

She seems worried to me. Too quiet. Almost sad.

"Something bothering you, Clara?" I ask. I guess it's all right for mothers to be nosey.

She heaves a deep sigh. "It's nothing, really." She tries to put on a brighter face. Then suddenly, she's crying and crushing herself into me. I hush-hush her, hugging her tightly as she sobs.

When she regains her composure and has dried her eyes, she says, "Sorry, Ma. Got carried away."

"What is it?" I ask. "You can tell me."

She shrugs. "Oh, I'm probably imagining things." She pauses. "I think Ben is having an affair."

"Really? What makes you think that?"

Another shrug. "I don't know. He doesn't seem the same anymore. Less loving, maybe. Works late more. Something."

I give her a big hug. "Well, don't look for trouble. He may have worries on his mind and keeps them to himself. Just take it easy; give him room."

Clara nods. Aaron wakes up and runs out of his room straight to his mother. She raises him into her arms.

"My, my, Aaron," she says, smiling at him, "you're getting so big that soon Mommy won't be able to pick you up!"

CHAPTER 22

Paul thinks we should mind our own business and not involve ourselves in whatever is going on between Clara and Ben. But that's not how I see it, and we have a serious argument. He gets angry, the way he was when I screwed up with the FBI.

"You never listen!" he shouts at me. "That's why you get into all these messes!"

Just what "all these messes" means I don't know, but I clam up, and the argument is over. It takes two to argue.

But bless his soul, Paul does get involved. He tells me, a few days later, that he has had lunch with Ben, who told him he was just having problems at work, nothing more. Paul accepted that as the reason for Ben's behavior. I listen, but I think he's wrong.

A week later, Clara is hysterical when she calls. Ben has been arrested and is in jail! His employer, National Bank, is accusing him of embezzlement. Now we know what "problems at work" meant.

It seems that Ben has been siphoning off small sums of money from every wire transfer received and accumulating them in a separate account—his. It's a simple stunt, and unlikely to be detected without a major audit. Just how long he thought he'd get away with it is a good question; maybe he wasn't thinking long-term.

Ben doesn't want Paul to defend him; he's too ashamed. But Clara asks Paul to take the case, and Ben yields.

The judge sets bail at $200,000. Clara doesn't have it, so we bail Ben out, between a bondsman and a second mortgage on our Bel Air house. We do it for Clara.

———

Ben's trial is scheduled for two months later. We hardly see him during that time. He goes into hiding. Clara is holding herself together rather well. We see Clara and the baby regularly. I love watching him grow.

The trial lasts less than a month. The prosecutor has mountains of evidence to prove what Ben has done. Paul has little to offer as a defense. None, in fact. He puts a few character witnesses on the stand. Thank God he doesn't include me!

The jury finds Ben guilty. His sentence, handed down the following month, is eight years in prison. Paul says he's surprised it's so light. To Clara, it must be a lifetime.

I ask her if she would like to move in with us. She is quick to accept. It's a happy Granny when Aaron and Clara become our "guests" in Bel Air.

Chapter 23

We visit Ben in the California State Prison in Sacramento. The "we" consists mostly of Carla and myself. Ben seems to have no interest in seeing Aaron, but Aaron keeps asking. "Me go see Daddy?" so we take him along a few times. Paul never makes the trip, and wants nothing to do with Ben, although he has filed the routine appeals. His feelings against his son-in-law have hardened since he discovered that Ben stole from the bank to play the horses. I ask him not to tell Clara, but I wonder if she already knows. After the first year of Ben's sentence, she seems to be visiting him out of a sense of duty, not enduring love.

Living with us provides Clara the opportunity to resume her film career. Once again, she is much sought after to direct major movies, and her name is on the list of top directors. Two of her films are nominated for best picture at the Oscars, and she wins for best director one year. The Directors' Guild has honored her several times.

She asks if she can invite a friend to dinner, and wants us to meet him. *Him?* I'm surprised, but say she certainly can. "*Mi casa, su casa.*" I probably have that wrong—not good with languages. I wonder who the friend could be.

Jason Phillips is one of Hollywood's big-name actors, known mostly for the action movies in which he stars. He is a towering, muscular giant, with a handshake like steel. But he is pleasant to talk to, laughs heartily, and is something of a gourmet. He and Chef Francois babble about various dishes; yes, Phillips speaks French fluently!

Within ten minutes, while we're having cocktails before dinner, I can see that Clara is very taken with Jason Phillips. She can't keep her eyes off him, and hangs on his every word. I'm sure she's not the first woman to fall in love with this extremely attractive man.

Chef Francois outdoes himself by serving *coq au vin* with Lyonnaise potatoes, and *chocolate mousse* for dessert. We have coffee in the living room, and gab on about movies till way into the night. Jason looks at his watch. "Holy smoke!" he says. "I have an early call; gotta get going!"

We say our good-byes at the door. Jason kisses Clara, hugs her gently.

Paul goes off to bed. Clara and I have another coffee.

"What do you think about Jason?" she asks.

"Quite a guy," I reply.

"Yes, he certainly is," Clara murmurs. "I like him a lot."

I smile. I'm happy for her, and glad she has a man in her life again.

CHAPTER 24

Clara tells me she wants to divorce Ben so she and Jason can marry. Now I'm really, really happy for her! I hug her. "How soon?" I ask.

"Like yesterday!" she says.

She goes off to Reno, and when she returns, divorce papers in hand, she tells me that she and Jason will get married as soon as he finishes the film being shot in Africa. In the meantime, we are to put together the guest list, reserve a nonreligious location, prepare invitations, find a gown for her, plan a reception—lots of work to keep us busy.

I ask Clara if she intends to see Ben one last time, to inform him of the divorce. She says that isn't necessary. Aside from the fact that she has no desire to see him, she says a copy of the divorce will be sent to him. I think it will make lousy reading in prison. What a shame their marriage fell apart the way it did.

Clara has some details to take care of for the last film she directed, dubbing dialogue that didn't suit the producers. She is off at a sound studio when Jason calls the house. He wants to tell Clara that they are scrambling to another location, because a civil war has suddenly broken out where they are shooting. I don't know the name of the studio where Clara is working, so I can't tell him where to reach her, if he wants to speak directly with her. He asks would I just tell her for him; he has to "hit the road and get the hell out of here."

By the time I get through to Clara, the war Jason mentioned is on the TV news, in confusing reports of what's happening. All I can make out is that rebel fighters are shelling the regime's capital. I relay Jason's message to her. She is on her way home, she tells me, instantly worried.

———◦◦◦◦◦◦◦———

She is increasingly worried when we have no further word from Jason for two days. His production company in Hollywood doesn't have anything new either, when Clara calls. But a TV news flash says fierce fighting continues in whatever the damned country it is.

A later news program shows rebel forces "taking prisoner several members of an American film crew," and Clara says she recognizes Jason! We watch another news program, and they have still more pictures. We both see Jason, a giant standing above the soldiers holding him prisoner. It looks to me like the kind of action movie Jason usually makes! Aaron is watching, and he shouts, "Jay-jay! Mama, Jay-jay!" He never mentions Daddy. "Jay-jay" is the one who swings him through the air, who tosses him up like a balloon, who puts him up on his shoulder to look down on the world.

Days go by without anymore news. That war has been re-placed by reports of still another uprising. "Jason's war" is soon history. We keep watching the news, hopeful and anxious.

Jason calls! The connection crackles and fades in and out, but I hear him say, "It's me, Jason." I quickly pass the phone to Clara.

"Jason! Oh, Jason!" is all she can say. The phone breaks up his next words, and then goes dead.

Another day passes, and then Jason calls again. This time his voice is loud and clear. He says he's in England and will be on the first plane he can make. Clara cries for joy. "Ja-jay is coming home!" she tells Aaron, hugging him tightly.

Chapter 25

We are all at LAX, waiting for Jason to arrive, little Aaron jumping up and down, singing "Jay-jay is coming home!" endlessly. It seems like hours after his plane lands before we catch sight of his head above the crowds surrounding him. When he breaks into the clear, he's in a wheelchair, a blanket covering his legs!

Clara reaches him first. He opens his arms to receive her. They remain that way for a long time, while Aaron tugs at him, calling "Jay-jay!" over and over. I stand nearby, pale and trembling. Finally, the airline attendant who has been taking care of Jason pushes the wheelchair to our car, Aaron bouncing and singing beside him. The attendant helps Jason struggle into the car. Jason doesn't have the use of his legs.

He is cheery and vocal as I drive us home. He is the first to say anything about his condition. We are settled in the living room. I am exhausted from struggling him into the house.

"I stepped on a bomb under the road," he says. "A wonder I wasn't blown to bits."

He pieces together the events leading up to the explosion, how he and two of his film crew escape their captors and flee into a deserted town. He doesn't know how long he lies on the ground before the Red Cross finds him.

Jason swallows a handful of pills, and we put him to bed.

Clara snuggles beside him. Early the next morning, a veterans' hospital ambulance picks him up.

———⁓∘⊶⊙⟋⊙⊶∘⁓———

Ben hangs himself in his prison cell. When the warden notifies Clara, she bends her head and cries. "The divorce papers," she says, "he must have just received them." She sobs, and then dries her eyes. "Poor man," she sighs. We accept the warden's offer, and Ben's body is driven down from Sacramento. Aaron asks, and I tell him it's his father in the coffin. His little lips form "Oh," and he sadly turns away. Clara and I see that Ben has a proper burial. I'm sure we have violated every rule in his religion's book.

———⁓∘⊶⊙⟋⊙⊶∘⁓———

Jason remains at the VA hospital in Westwood, where Clara visits him daily, sometimes with Aaron, often with me. The giant that was Jason seems to have become just one more damaged soldier among the many we see there. How ironic, I think, for Jason to have escaped injury on two tours in Iraq, only to become crippled while filming a stupid movie.

Yet no one at the hospital is in better spirits than Jason. He undergoes several surgeries to repair spinal damage, but the verdict remains the same: he will be a paraplegic for the rest of his life. He accepts it, and even before he is released, he is making plans to pick up the pieces and move on.

Now we have two film directors in the family. Jason starts directing a film similar to the action movies that had made him a star. But Clara doesn't go to work. She devotes herself to Aaron, and is much too protective, I think, as though her mission in life is to care for the men in it. She looks after Jason, who lives with us, whenever he's not off somewhere shooting a film. No one mentions the marriage that almost happened.

CHAPTER 26

I decide to go to work. This life of leisure in Bel Air is boring the hell out of me. But I want to avoid the old corporate rat race. And I will have nothing to do with the movie business.

When I mention my dilemma to Paul, he says, "Have you thought of going back to college, getting a master's, even a PhD?"

I scoff at his suggestion, but after awhile, I find myself toying with an idea related to it. What if I *started* a college or university? But not just another university, a special kind—*for people with handicaps like Jason's!*

The idea takes root, and Paul is an instant backer. Clara is enthusiastic, too. I begin reading up on state requirements for accreditation of institutions of higher learning. Soon I am placing advertisements for faculty members in the *Atlantic*, the *Journal of the London School of Economics*, the *Financial Times*, and other publications with educational readership (having consulted media reference books in the public library in Beverly Hills).

I receive more resumes and inquiries than I can possibly handle by myself, so I have an employment agency find me a secretary—excuse me—an administrative assistant. After several interviews, I hire Margaret Flynn, a very capable redhead who takes steno, knows PowerPoint, Excel, Word, a flock of other programs, and is lightning on a computer keyboard.

Maggie (as she prefers) and I begin culling through stacks of resumes and responding to telephone inquiries.

Within a few days, I am interviewing potential faculty members for my university: Martin Brackett, who has a Pulitzer for his work in behavioral science; Elaine Mullins, PhD in American literature; and William Scott Norton, physics (has nineteen patents)—people of that order, wanting to be a part of this unusual educational idea. I also meet with California education authorities in Sacramento, gathering information on rules and practices.

"What's your university's name going to be?" Paul asks. He has earlier advised against using the word "handicapped" in any way. Of course!

I tell him I'm still working on it. It's the least of my problems at the moment. But then, suddenly, I think I've got it! If he's willing to lend his name, I would call it the Jason Dermott Phillips University of California.

"I like!" Paul exclaims when I try the name out on him. "Go! Go!"

Jason requires some persuasion, showing unexpected modesty for a movie star, but soon agrees. I think little Aaron agrees, too, even though he doesn't have a clue as to what we're talking about.

———

Two years later, construction of our new university's buildings and campus is complete, on three hundred priceless acres overlooking the Pacific Ocean, donated by the city of Santa Monica.

That fall marks the first semester of the Jason Dermott Phillips University of California. There is just one unusual requirement for student admission: a physical impairment of some kind.

Casey Calhoun is president.

CHAPTER 27

It's not often that an educational institution makes headline news without being the site of a shooting massacre. The Phillips University, as it has become known, appears on the front pages of the *New York Times*, the *Chicago Tribune*, the *London Times*, and just about every newspaper in the United States and many foreign countries. *Time* gives it a cover and an inside pull-out section. Scott Pelley and Leslie Stahl interview Jason, me, two faculty members, and three students in a one-hour *60 Minutes* special. Their pictures of the campus show students in wheelchairs, others with one arm or none, and many whose artificial limbs are concealed by clothing.

A popular morning TV host thinks it's funny to say the campus looks like a convalescent home for wounded veterans.

Maggie Flynn asks me, "What about sports? Is that a possibility?"

I say I hadn't thought about it, but in no time, I'm talking with athletic directors of colleges and high schools. I lure Mickey Williams, athletic director and basketball coach at Santa Monica High, to sign up with us and develop an athletic program tailored to fit our students.

I give Maggie a raise.

—⁓⁘⁜⁘⁜⁘⁓—

At the start of the second year, Phillips enrollment increases to 3,201 students, and the costs of operations, including faculty payroll, gardeners, maintenance crews, and building repairs, have gone through the roof. Our tuition has been the lowest of any four-year institution, but that will have to change radically, unless we can get a number of scholarships, and outright donations from wealthy philanthropists.

I go after some of the richest people in Los Angeles, Orange County, and northern California. Eli Broad, whose name is on several art museums in LA, readily commits to a whopping $2 million annual donation. He is soon joined by two other donors who wish to remain anonymous. Problem solved: Phillips has an annual endowment of $7 million! *Ask and ye shall be heard.* I read that somewhere.

CHAPTER 28

P aul has been itching to participate in the Phillips venture from the start, but his law firm has kept him too busy to take on any additional responsibilities. Of course, he is ready to assist us with legal representation when needed, such as drawing up contracts, putting endowments in writing, defending the university in any suits, but he wants to be more deeply involved.

No sooner said than done. I suggest he have his partners buy him out and chair a Law Department at Phillips, developing courses to be added to the syllabus.

"Now why didn't I think of that!" Paul exclaims. "Thanks, Case!"

Clara has been as busy taking care of little Aaron as I have building a university, but he's ready for preschool, giving Clara some time of her own. It's not enough time for her to start working again, but enables her to see old movie friends, and have some kind of life besides mother.

When Jason returns from the film he is working on at the end of the day (he drives a car with hand controls and a tricky way for him to climb behind the wheel), I am pleased to hear Clara contribute to their conversation—about actors and producers she has seen, sets she has visited, dailies she has screened, Hollywood gossip. But I can tell she'd love to be directing again.

I think it's high time she had a serious break. Phillips is doing fine, and can get along without Casey Calhoun, president, for a while. I hand over the reins to Dr. Herman Goode, my provost, and assume charge of Aaron. He is in school half the day, so I also have a few hours to myself. Clara has the whole day to spend in Hollywood or wherever. She may run into Jason.

I use the time when I'm alone at the Bel Air house to put the story of Phillips University down on paper. Every morning, as soon as Aaron leaves on the school bus, I'm at my laptop. And while Aaron takes his midday nap, or is playing with his toys when we're out at the pool, my fingers are clicking away at the keyboard.

I'm so proud of what I've written; I show the first fifty pages to Clara. She loves what she reads, and says, "I wish I could make such good use of my time!" That encourages me to work even harder at the computer.

When I have another fifty or so pages, I show the manuscript to Paul, who says, "That is one helluva story, Casey. I had no idea you could write so well!" Jason's reaction is along the same lines, although he thinks I've given him far too much space (such modesty from a movie star!).

I am out at the pool with Aaron one afternoon, pounding away at the laptop, and pause to dash into the house for another pitcher of iced tea. When I return, I don't see Aaron on the grass where he had been playing. His big red-and-white ball is floating on the water.

"Aaron!" I shriek, and dive into the pool. I find him at the bottom, seize his limp body, and carry him up and out of the pool.

I lay him face down and frantically try to resuscitate him with all I know. After one last mouth-to-mouth attempt, I collapse. Moments later, I call 911, but I know there's nothing they can do. My little Aaron is gone.

CHAPTER 29

Aaron's funeral is the worst day of my life. I haven't stopped crying since the moment I pulled him out of the pool; nor have I looked even once into Clara's face. She hasn't spoken a word to me. I vaguely hear the pastor speak.

When his little white coffin is lowered into the grave, my anguish becomes so severe that I can't breathe. I black out, and collapse where I stand. Someone puts bitter smelling salts under my nose. I sputter and cough as Paul helps me to my feet.

Clara moves out of the house. I've lost her again. My laptop has gone to the city dump in the trash truck, along with my unfinished manuscript. I lie in bed most of the time. I never go near the pool.

Paul has tried his best to comfort me, but nothing he says or does can ever wash away what I have done. I haven't said anything to the people at Phillips—Paul has taken care of it, he tells me.

He puts the Bel Air house into a Realtor's hands and goes about preparations for our moving out. I don't ask where we're going. It turns out to be the Beverly Wilshire Hotel. Paul checks us in. I hear him say he reserved a suite on the lowest floor available.

Must be afraid I would jump out of a window. If only it was that easy.

———— ✦ ————

Months go by. I'm much better. At least I walk around, talk to people, look normal, and smile now and then. It's November, but Beverly Hills already has Christmas lights across Wilshire Boulevard and on the palm trees. The hotel has its Christmas awnings up. Paul suggests we have lunch at Cut, the Puck restaurant in the hotel. I shake my head, remembering how Puck embarrassed me by saying I was the one who got canned at Trinitrion. I say, "How about Nate 'n' Al's?"

I must be getting better. I even laugh once at something Paul says. But I rarely have a good night's sleep. My nightmare will never leave me. How I wish Clara would talk with me again!

———— ✦ ————

Paul wants to take us on a trip somewhere. Maybe China, he suggests. I don't care, but I think traveling might help me—a different scene. I can see that Paul hasn't given up on me yet. He's all I have left.

CHAPTER 30

Christmas Day is tomorrow. We are still at the Beverly Wilshire. The "trip" never happens. Paul has gone out to see his former law firm partners several times. He isn't afraid to let me be alone anymore. I know he's thinking of going back to work.

We spend Christmas Eve in our suite, and have the hotel's fabulous Christmas dinner spread out in our dining room, turkey and all the trimmings. I think we did the same on Thanksgiving Day but can't quite recall. My memory must be going.

In my dreams that night, little Aaron is walking jauntily across a street with me, holding my hand. He's wearing the blue jumpsuit I gave him for his last birthday. How was I to know it would really be his *last* one? At least I don't have that terrible poolside nightmare anymore.

Paul hasn't been seeing his former partners every time he goes out, he confesses at dinner one evening. He has also been to see Clara, on the set where she is working on a film, and once at Lombardo's, a Hollywood lunch eatery. He says he thinks her attitude toward me is softening; she doesn't sound so bitter or angry.

I'm happy to hear this, but I still don't think I can face her, if that's what Paul is working toward. He shrugs. "Let's see how it goes."

———— ∾◦◦∾◦◦∾ ————

Jason phones. I haven't seen him in a long time, and when he asks if he could have dinner with Paul and me, I readily make the date. We'll meet at the Bel Air Hotel. My demons sure have backed off!

Clara is behind Jason's wheelchair when Marcel shows them to our table. No one says a word, except the maitre d', wishing us *bon appetite* as he hands out menus.

I sneak a peek at Clara over the top of my menu. Her face is almost gaunt; she has lost even more weight. Her eyes meet mine, and I see sadness in just a fleeting moment. I regret making the date with Jason. I should have suspected what he was up to.

Jason talks about the university. He has visited Phillips while a volleyball game was in progress between teams of wheelchair-bound students. He describes other sports the university has developed for different impairments. I give myself a gold star for getting Mikey Williams to join Phillips as athletic director.

Paul talks about a plagiarism case his old law firm is handling.

"Someone stole a writer's book?" Clara asks, her first words of the evening, and I sense a sarcasm in her tone. I am increasingly uncomfortable. I want to leave, right then, but we are almost finished, so I sit tight. Paul has caught all of this and calls for the check. We get our coats and go out, wait for our cars to be brought around. Our "good nights" are quick. Jason shakes hands with Paul, and thanks him. I lean into Jason to plant a light kiss on his cheek. Clara helps him up behind the wheel.

I wonder what was accomplished as Paul drives us home to the hotel. I guess seeing Clara could be called an accomplishment, all things considered. Maybe her door is open just a crack.

CHAPTER 31

Spring arrives, and with the budding trees comes an invitation
to attend the wedding of Jason and Clara. I am so surprised,
my heart beating so hard, I have to sit down. I call Paul, who has
been working off-and-on with his former partners. He expresses
surprise, but something tells me he already knows.

Maybe he also knows that Clara is pregnant. She phones me,
says she has to find a maternity wedding gown. I think her calling
is a sign that things are okay again. I'm happy to help. *I'm happy!*

The wedding takes place on the campus of Phillips
University—on a great stretch of green lawn used for commence-
ment exercises. It's a simple affair. Bishop Thomas McCarran, of
First AME Church, blesses us all and performs the brief cere-
mony. His church's gospel choir of maybe fifty women wearing
big, wide-brimmed hats breaks into the wildest dancing and singing I've ever witnessed.

But we were wedding guests, that's all. To say that Clara and
I are now reconciled would be a gross overstatement. She has
called me just once since the wedding, and only to ask the name

of my gynecologist. I can see that she doesn't care for me to be in touch. It hurts.

She goes to Cedars-Sinai to have a Caesarian birth. She must have planned it this way. We receive a card announcing the arrival of Charles Theodore Phillips, weighing 5½ pounds. I return the formality by simply having Macy's ship a stroller to her.

I see Charles for the first time three months later, when Clara appears at the hotel, baby in the stroller. No hug, not even a hello. She offers no reason for the surprise visit, accepts my offer of tea. We sit in the living room and watch Charles on the floor. He is already crawling, of a sort, and will surely walk early. He is big, taking after Jason. I study Clara. Her expression gives me the feeling that she is detached from her child, as if she's afraid to show her love. The loss of Aaron must still haunt her, as it does me.

<hr />

Jason calls to invite us to a house-warming party at their new home in Brentwood, in the best section, above Montana Avenue. It's a big house, four bedrooms, a full dining room, great kitchen, spacious patio. Three-car garage. Wonderful lawn in the back. No pool.

Clara meets us at the door when we arrive. Without a hug or a welcoming smile, she accepts the flowers we've brought, and goes off to put them in a vase. She pays little attention to me all evening. Paul and I mingle, knowing many of the guests from Phillips. He has a good time. I am confused.

Next day, I drive to the lot where Jason is working, and when there's a break, I go up to him at the food table. He's glad to see me, and reaches up from his wheelchair to give me a great hug.

"How's it going?" I ask, to start us talking. I really don't know what I came to say.

"No complaints," he says, buttering a bagel, "other than little Charlie keeps us up all night."

I'm glad he thinks I'm asking about home, not work. "Clara? She okay?"

He shrugs, his expression thoughtful. "Not so hot, really. She's been to the doctor a couple of times. I think he's your guy."

I remember her asking for my gynecologist's name. Jason sees I'm waiting for more information, and adds, "Oh, nothing serious, or she'd tell me. Not to worry, Casey."

———✦———

At first, Dr. Berger is reluctant to talk about another patient, but seeing that Clara is my daughter, he reveals that she has problems with her uterus, and it may have to be removed, which was why she had the Caesarian.

"Things go wrong," he says with a shrug. "Let's hope it doesn't lead to worse problems."

As I leave his office, I decide it's up to me to break the barrier between Clara and me. I'm her mother. I sadly recall how furious she was when she first learned I'm the mother who abandoned her in Switzerland.

I take a chance. Without calling, I drive to Brentwood and find Clara sitting on the lawn at the rear of her house, sipping iced tea and reading a paperback. Charles is so thoroughly occupied with building a fortress out of Lego bricks that he doesn't look up when I say, "Hello! Anybody home?"

Clara puts her book aside and comes toward me. I am almost stunned when she puts her arms around me and hugs me tightly. I press my lips to her cheek. It's moist from the tears flowing from her eyes.

"Ma, Ma," she murmurs. When we separate, she says, crumpling a tissue to her nose, "I've been such a fool."

I put my arms around her waist and just look at her. Charles has left his fortress to come over and watch us, a puzzled expression on his face.

"Charlie," Clara tells him, "say hello to your grandma."

He isn't sure what he is supposed to do. "Hi, Granny," he says. "Want to see my fort?" He takes my hand and leads me to the half-built structure. I smooth his dark, rumpled hair. *Granny?* It is the sweetest word I've ever heard.

CHAPTER 32

Clara is in recovery at Cedars-Sinai when Dr. Berger and a hospital physician approach me in the waiting room. I've been sitting there for hours, having driven over as soon as Jason calls. He goes back to work when told it would be a long wait.

"She's doing fine," my gynecologist says. The other physician nods, saying, "You'll be able to see her in an hour or so, when the anesthetics wear off."

Jason returns, and we wait for almost two hours before we can go to her room. She's wan and tired, but gives us a brave smile. A nurse tells us not to stay too long, the patient should get some sleep.

"Sorry to give you all so much trouble," Clara says.

I pat her hand. "No trouble, Clara. You rest now. I'll come back tomorrow."

Jason raises up from his wheelchair to kiss her cheek, and we leave.

———

Jason surprises me by calling to see if he can come up. He's in the lobby. Clara is back in their home, a nurse staying with her for a few days.

He wheels into my living room, and we have coffee. He is groping for words, I think, as we sit quietly.

"I have a problem," he says, fidgeting with his shirtsleeve. "Clara and I were updating our wills, which you're supposed to do regularly."

He pauses.

"Clara," he continues, "has added a codicil that says that if anything happens to her and me, Charlie is to be given to her friend, Anita Welsh, to adopt, and under no circumstances given to Casey Calhoun Ellsworth."

He takes a deep breath. "She insists that I put the same thing in my will. I don't want to. I hate to be fighting with her when she's just out of the hospital."

I am speechless. I thought all that rancor was behind us now. Apparently not.

"Well," I say, "you'll have to work it out between you, but it hurts to think she feels that way about me."

Jason mumbles that he's sorry, and after we sit a while more, he hugs me good-bye and wheels out to the elevator.

CHAPTER 33

Anita Welsh is a name I have not heard before, but if she's to adopt Charles, I have to find out who she is. Google tells me everything. Anita Welsh is an eighth-grade teacher at Wellington Elementary in Brentwood. She is president of the Gay, Lesbian, and Transgender Coalition.

I am startled. But I realize that somebody could have a lesbian friend without being one herself, so I don't jump to conclusions. I decide to visit this Anita Welsh.

She knows who I am when I phone, and she says, "Sure, come on over."

Her address turns out to be an apartment house in Brentwood, below Wilshire, second floor. She is a short, heavy brunette with flabby arms. She shakes my hand, and ushers me into her small apartment. We have coffee in her living room, and she starts the conversation by asking, "How is Clara doing? I didn't get a chance to visit her in the hospital, but I understand she's home now?"

I reply that Clara is doing fine, and will be up and around in no time. "Oh, great!" she exclaims. "Maybe she'll make the gay parade next week, if she's up to it. She hasn't missed one in years."

I'm totally confused, and I drive to the studio where Jason is working. At the next break, I ask him how well he knows Anita Welsh.

"She's Clara's friend," he says, "I don't think I've ever met her. All I know is Clara's been seeing her for years. They were in school together."

"Did you know she's a lesbian?" I ask.

"No, really? Clara never said." Jason thinks for a while. "No, she never mentioned it to me."

As he starts to wheel back to work, he says, "Oh, just so you know, I'm not putting that thing Clara wanted in my will."

———

Paul says, when I tell him all about it, "Depends on who goes first. Just hope it's not Clara."

That's no help.

Chapter 34

C lara has been home from the hospital for over a month. She looks good, has gained back some of the weight she lost, and is up and about more actively than ever. When I visit her, she is affable and seems glad to see me. I want to bring up the will matter that has been clouding my mind ever since Jason told me about it, but I can't find a way to say a word without causing trouble between them. And the lesbian thing, with Anita Welsh—that's another thing nagging me.

Jason is on the phone, agitated. He tells me that when he comes home that night, the house is dark and empty. He looks for a note on the fridge door—nothing there. Disturbed, since it's quite late, he wheels about the house, and finds only empty hangers in her clothes closet, empty drawers in her dresser. Charlie's things are gone, too, toys and all.

He sounds ready to break down. "Jason," I say, "I'll be right over!" and buzz down to the concierge to have my car brought around quickly. I wish Paul was home, but it's his poker night, something he's been doing lately. I drive to Brentwood, and find a desolate Jason in a cold house.

"Why?" he asks, "Why would she run off like this? It's crazy!"

Something that has been on my mind finds a voice. "Let me

make a call." I have Anita Welsh's number in my iPhone, but my call goes to voice mail.

"Let's take a ride, Jason," I tell him. We have to go in his car; I could never lift him up into mine. He gets behind the wheel.

"Where to?"

I give him directions, right turn, left turn, go straight, until I tell him to stop in front of an apartment house.

"Wait here," I say, and go into the building. I find Anita Welsh's button, press it, get no response. I press the super's button, and an angry voice shouts from the intercom, "Who the hell's calling this time of night!"

"Sorry," I answer, "got an emergency, have to find Anita Welsh!"

"She ain't here!" he yells. "She took off this afternoon, bag and baggage, like she's never coming back, the goddamned lesbo!"

I thank him and go out to Jason. I get into the car. Jason looks at me.

"Clara's gone off with Anita Welsh," I tell him. "Charlie's with her."

He stares at me for a long time before turning on the engine. Not a word is said as he drives me back to the Beverly Wilshire.

CHAPTER 35

F ive months pass and no word from Clara. I've put my detective agency to work, McFadden is on the case, but they get nowhere, not even a lead. It's as though Clara, her friend, and Charlie have dropped off the planet.

McFadden calls. "Bad news, Casey," he says. "Police in Hawaii have a body that washed ashore at Maui. Sorry, but they've identified her as Clara Phillips. No question."

I am stunned, totally freaked out. How I manage to tell Jason, I'll never know. He takes the news with almost no reaction, as though he has been expecting it all along. I also tell him they are still looking for Anita Welsh and little Charlie. He seems indifferent.

───────

Jason asks us, Paul and me, to come live with him in his Brentwood house. We have tired of hotel living, aside from the dent it makes in our finances, and readily accept. I'll miss having everything done for me, but I'll get along.

I like being in a house again. It's nothing compared with our old Bel Air mansion, but it's comfortable, very livable. I wouldn't go near a swimming pool anyway. Jason seems to enjoy our company. And the breakfasts I prepare for him. He never mentions Clara or Charlie.

Jason is a busy man. He has directed two major films in the past two years, one nominated for Best Picture Oscar, and he has a Best Director Oscar. He still teaches a popular film class at Phillips.

———————

McFadden has a lead. A Crayton affiliate in Tokyo has run across a photo composite (sent out to agents and casting people) of a little boy who bears a remarkable resemblance to Charlie—older, of course, than the last picture of the missing boy.

McFadden says he's looking into it, will get back to me when he has more to report.

Japan! If it is Charlie, Anita Welsh is certainly moving around. She must think we've given up anyway, and is now trying to make a buck by having Charlie become a child actor.

That gives me an idea. I ask Jason for the names of some casting services in Hollywood, and go to Margaret Lipton Associates to look through their books of actors' photos. They are very helpful when I tell them my story. But after a full day of flipping thousands of pages, scanning God knows how many photos, I give up. No Charlie. Just for the heck of it, I look for Anita Welsh, too. No Anita, either. Well, it was worth a try.

———————

The police in Hawaii have stayed on the case, McFadden tells me, and a second autopsy of Clara's corpse has revealed evidence that changes the cause of death from accidental drowning to homicide. She had suffered a fatal blow to her brain before being tossed into the sea. Now the hunt is on in earnest for the woman who was last seen with a small boy.

In Japan, the Crayton affiliate reports to McFadden that they have interviewed people who remember seeing a woman with a boy, and they are now zeroing in on a particular house.

"They've got him!" McFadden exclaims in his next call. "The Tokyo police have found Charlie!" But Anita Welsh is still at large.

———————

Charlie is brought back to Los Angeles by an operative of the Crayton Tokyo affiliate. The little boy I remember has grown considerably, I see, as Jason and I meet him at LAX. He shows no recognition of us, but goes with us to his father's car, and we drive home.

He goes with me to the mall in Century City, where he picks out a whole new wardrobe, including a T-shirt reading Born to Be Free. He looks like a regular kid, but there's something solemn about him. He can talk when he wants to, but he's mostly silent.

I enroll him in the nearest elementary school, in the second grade, feeling like a mother. The questions asked about his mother during the enrollment prompt him to question me later.

"Was she a nice lady?" he asks, over cookies and milk. "Did she wear pretty dresses?" He thinks. "I remember Nita better."

I avoid even mentioning Anita Welsh, but I am pleased when McFadden reports that she is finally in custody in Tokyo, and is being extradited to Hawaii to stand trial. "First degree murder," he says.

Her defense attorney has me served with a subpoena. Paul says I have to go; that's the law. He talks to the attorney, lawyer to lawyer, and finds I'm an important witness in Anita's defense. Paul agrees to go with me to Hawaii, like taking a vacation. Jason says he and Charlie will be fine, not to worry. He'll show him how movies are made.

We are packed and ready to leave for LAX when McFadden calls. *Anita Welsh hanged herself in her cell last night.* I am shocked by the brutal sound of the news and realize that now we will never know what happened when Anita Welsh disappeared with Clara and Charlie.

But I am greatly relieved as I unpack my luggage. Paul pretends to be disappointed by the cancellation of his "vacation" in Hawaii.

With all that now behind us, we settle down as one solid family. I will raise Charlie as a combined mother and granny. Jason will see his son become a man. Paul is the protector of us all. I will keep Clara in my heart forever.

EPILOGUE

I vy covers many walls at Phillips University, and it no longer limits enrollment to those with physical impairment. Charles (he refuses to be called Charlie) has a bachelor of science degree from Phillips, completed his premed at UCLA, and became an MD after three years at NYU's Medical School. He heads the gynecology department at Cedars-Sinai.

We lost Jason. Certain internal problems caused by the bomb that made him a paraplegic finally ended his life. His memorial is the university he helped build.

Paul and I are old and gray and still share the love that so many obstacles could have destroyed. The Law Library at Phillips bears his name.

Secretly, though, I still think of myself as Casey Calhoun, the girl who once slept her way to the top.

Printed in the United States
By Bookmasters